Merry Christmas 1994
Sydney
Love
Alexandra & ADDISON

Why Ducks Sleep on One Leg

BY SHERRY GARLAND

ILLUSTRATED BY JEAN AND
MOU-SIEN TSENG

SCHOLASTIC INC.
New York

To Phoebe Yeh—
thanks for your hard work
and encouragement.
S.G.

Library of Congress Cataloging-in-Publication Data

Garland, Sherry.
Why ducks sleep on one leg / written by Sherry Garland:
illustrated by Jean and Mou-sien Tseng.
p. cm.
Summary: A Vietnamese folktale explains the phenomenon
of ducks sleeping on one leg.
ISBN 0-590-45697-0
[1. Ducks—Folklore. 2. Folklore—Vietnam.] I. Tseng, Jean,
ill. II. Tseng, Mou-sien, ill. III. Title.
PZ8.1.G1668Wh 1993
398.2—dc20
[E] 92-9709
CIP
AC

12 11 10 9 8 7 6 5 4 3 2 1 3 4 5 6 7 8/9

Printed in the U.S.A. 36

First Scholastic printing, February 1993

Designed by Claire B. Counihan

The illustrations in this book are
watercolor paintings.

Author's Note

Việt-Nam (VEE-et Nahm) is an ancient land in Southeast Asia whose culture goes back almost four thousand years. It was first occupied by nomadic tribes, then by the Viets who originally came from a region of southern China. For thousands of years the primary belief of the people was animism. People worshipped the spirits of all things — rocks, trees, rivers, animals. This was their way of explaining natural phenomena and asking for good crops.

The Chinese conquered Việt-Nam in 111 B.C. and ruled for one thousand years. The conquerors introduced Confucianism, Taoism, Buddhism, and many aspects of Chinese culture. For a while, the upper-class Vietnamese adopted Chinese dress, and spoke and wrote Chinese. But, eventually, the Vietnamese combined their old beliefs and these new philosophies to create a unique culture with its own writing, dress, customs, and colorful legends and folktales.

The village in *Why Ducks Sleep on One Leg* is typical of those in ancient feudal Việt-Nam. The center of village life was the *đình* (dEEn), or communal house. It was the focal point for all civic activities and the place to worship the *thành-hoàng* (tahn hwahng) or, village guardian. He or she was often the village founder, or a famous local hero. The villagers believed this "god" or patron saint would bring them good luck and protection from danger.

Inside the *đình*, wooden tablets were inscribed with the name and deeds of the guardian.

Today, the *đình* are used during village ceremonies and festivals and as schools. They are also used for political meetings and as public health centers.

LONG, LONG AGO in the land of Việt-Nam, there was a time when animals could talk like humans. Dragons rode to earth on clouds of rain, and unicorns frolicked in the woods. Fairies dwelled on misty mountains, and in every rock, tree, and stream, there lived a magic spirit. During this time of wonder, the ruler of all gods and spirits was Ngọc Hoàng, the Jade Emperor.

The earth was young then. All the animals were newly created, boasting feathers and fur, fins and feet. And they were content—except for three ducks who lived in a small rice-farming village. These unhappy ducks had received only one leg each.

Now the ducks were clever, so they soon noticed that something was very wrong. When they tried to dive for fish, they couldn't paddle and almost drowned. When they found worms on the ground, the hens always beat them to it. And if the unlucky ducks didn't get out of his way quickly, the clumsy water buffalo stepped on them.

The three ducks managed as best they could. They held each other's wings for balance when they walked. They took turns watching out for hungry foxes and pythons. And they shared their food with each other. But when the other animals teased them, they became most resentful of their plight.

"It isn't fair that someone ran out of duck legs and forgot to make any more," said the oldest duck.

"That's right, sister," said the middle duck. "I'm tired of being hungry all the time."

"And I'm tired of those monkeys in the jungle making fun of us," said the youngest duck. "What can we do about it?"

"Let's petition the Jade Emperor for three more duck legs," suggested the oldest duck. "He's the ruler of heaven and earth. Surely he will help us."

The ducks borrowed a block of ink, a brush, and some rice paper.

"Now, which one of us will write the petition?" asked the oldest duck.

"I will," said the middle duck. "I know just what to say."

He sat under a banyan tree and began writing with a flourish. All day, all night, and all the next morning, he wrote while his sister and brother waited patiently.

"Oh, dear," said the oldest duck. "Your letter is so long. And you didn't even mention our missing legs."

"Why don't *you* write it, sister dear," replied the middle duck.

"I think we should ask the rooster for help," said the oldest duck. "He's always strutting about the village, bragging and crowing his royal connections. Maybe he's related to the Jade Emperor."

The ducks sought out the rooster, who was most eager to assist them. He drafted a petition on the spot.

"Now we have our petition," said the oldest duck. "Who wants to present it to the Jade Emperor?"

"Not I," said the middle duck. "I hear the emperor has an awful temper."

"Not I," said the youngest duck. "I don't know where he lives."

"Oh, that's easy," said their sister. "The Jade Emperor lives in the heavens beyond the sky. His Celestial Palace rests on the banks of the Silver River, whose waters twinkle with the brilliance of a million stars. You must cross the Rainbow Bridge to reach the celestial dogs who guard the palace gates. Only mandarins in the pursuit of study are allowed to stroll in the Garden of Fragrant Peonies and Flowering Peach Trees."

"Well, that sounds nice," said the middle duck. "But it's too far away. How can we walk to the Celestial Palace with only one leg each?"

"What if we get lost?" added the youngest duck.

"I suppose you're right," agreed the oldest duck. "And, besides," she whispered, "just look at the way the rooster wrote the petition. The characters look like scratch marks to me!"

The three ducks sadly huddled at the edge of the lotus pond. They heard someone clearing her throat. It was a goose standing nearby.

"Excuse me," the goose said. "I overheard you talking and I know how to help you. You should go to Thành-Hoàng, the village guardian spirit who lives in the *đình*. He visits the Jade Emperor all the time. Convince him to take your petition on his next journey to the Celestial Palace. I will write a letter of introduction to Thành-Hoàng myself."

The three ducks thanked the goose for her kindness and set out with her letter and the rooster's petition.

The ducks cut bamboo canes, and wove leaf-hats to shade their heads from the hot sun. The *đình* was at the other end of the village, which was a long trip for ducks with only one leg each.

Hours later, the ducks saw the curved tile roof of the *đình*. Carefully they wiped their feet and bowed three times before they entered the dark building. They smelled freshly lit candles, the sweet perfume of joss sticks, and bouquets of dahlias and lilies. They noticed bowls of luscious fruit piled high on the altar, but did not see a living soul. Then, from a back chamber, they heard a loud, angry voice.

"I told you the incense burner must have three legs. Why does this one have six? Remove the extra legs immediately! Take them out of my sight!"

The ducks put their heads close together.

"What is an incense burner?" asked the youngest duck.

"I don't know," replied the middle duck, "but it has three extra legs. Maybe they are the legs we never received!"

Thành-Hoàng entered the room. He towered over the ducks. His glare was frightful. "What do you want?" he demanded.

The oldest duck offered up the goose's letter of introduction. The guardian spirit hurriedly read aloud: "'I, most humble of geese, present to you, most honored of spirits, guardian of our village, hero of our hearts, protector of our fields and homes, these three unfortunate ducks, victims of a fate, most inequitable and malevolent, who beg you to consider their petition....'"

"All right, all right," grumbled the guardian spirit. "Show it to me."

Thành-Hoàng struggled to decipher the rooster's writing. Suddenly he burst into laughter. "Ducks with only one leg each? Preposterous!"

"Then you *will* carry our petition to the Jade Emperor?" asked the middle duck anxiously.

"Certainly not. Whatever was done at creation time cannot be undone. Obviously you were meant to have one leg each. Besides, the Jade Emperor would never admit a mistake was made. I cannot take your petition to him. It might make him angry at me." The guardian spirit callously threw the scroll aside.

The ducks fell into a gloomy silence. Finally, the youngest duck spoke out in his bravest voice...."Honored Spirit," said he, "when we came into the *đình,* we overheard you telling your servant to get rid of three extra legs. Perhaps we could have them."

"Extra legs? I have no extra duck legs here."

"Oh, they were not duck legs," said the oldest duck. "They were from the incense burner—whatever that is. But we are not picky ducks. Any leg is better than none."

"Those legs? They are pure gold!" Thành-Hoàng's laughter shook the roof tiles. "I suppose you can have them, but guard them carefully, or someone may steal them. And I have no more."

The ducks gratefully thanked Thành-Hoàng for his generosity. They bowed three times and quickly backed out of the *đình* before he could change his mind.

Once outside, the ducks tried on their golden legs. They fit perfectly.

Back at home, the ducks cheerfully showed off their new legs. "Watch me swim," shouted the oldest duck. She dived into the pond and gobbled up a goldfish.

"Watch me run," cried the middle duck. He raced into the yard and stole a worm from an unwary hen.

"Watch me fly," bragged the youngest duck. He leaped onto the broad back of a dumbfounded water buffalo and flapped his wings.

And so the ducks treasured their new golden legs. They ate as much as they liked and soon grew plump. But they never forgot Thành-Hoàng's warning. Each night, they tucked their golden legs up under their wings, safely out of sight.

As time passed, ducks visiting from villages near and far noticed this curious habit and followed suit. They discovered that standing on one leg was a comfortable way to sleep. At nightfall, they, too, began tucking their legs up under their wings. Over the years the custom spread throughout the world. And so it remains today.